One Night

for Diana Kidd,
who was a good friend
and a lovely writer

One Night

Margaret Wild

Alfred A. Knopf   New York

THIS IS A BORZOI BOOK PUBLISHED BY ALFRED A. KNOPF

www.randomhouse.com/teens

Library of Congress Cataloging-in-Publication Data
Wild, Margaret, 1948–
One night / Margaret Wild. — 1st American ed.
p.   cm.
SUMMARY: In this novel in free verse and narrated by alternating
characters, a teenaged girl decides to have her baby and care for it on her
own after a "one night stand" results in pregnancy.
ISBN 0-375-82920-2 (trade) — ISBN 0-375-92920-7 (lib. bdg.)
[1. Pregnancy—Fiction. 2. Teenage mothers—Fiction.] I. Title.
PZ7.W64574On2004
[Fic]—dc22   2003060619

Printed in the United States of America
May 2004
10   9   8   7   6   5   4   3   2   1
First American Edition

the parties

The parties were Bram's idea—
calculated,
sophisticated,
daring.
For a long time
they were the best-kept secret
in the city.
They ended
one night
when Al nearly killed Raphael.

Gabe

GABE ~ collecting girls

First Saturday in summer,
Johnstone Public Swimming Pool
now called
Johnstone Park Aquatic Center
to match its glitzy new image.
I'm sitting here, in my sunglasses,
checking the pool.
Target: collecting girls.

A surly waitress slaps down
a cappuccino, weak as cat's piss,
slopping into the saucer.
I give her my devastating smile,
and she stares at me,
mouth hanging open.
For a moment I consider coaxing
her into a smile,
but I can't waste time.
I turn to survey the poolside.
To the right the high-diving pool—
young boys jostling,
eager to show off.
Straight ahead the Olympic pool—
two lanes reserved for coaching.
To the left the heated pool,
and the little kids' pool.
Then the grassy banks
rolling down to the bay,
and clusters of girls and guys.

I dig out some coins
and leave them on the table.
I catch the waitress looking at me,
her face wistful.
I shouldn't have smiled.
Of course I could invite her
to the party tonight, but I don't want
the bother of looking after her.
Better not.

I saunter down the steps,
scan the main pool
for chicks on their own,
or with their girlfriends.
At the deep end, squealing,
are a couple of possibles.
I may come back to them later.

GABE ~ so bram says

Tonight the party will be
at Chris's house,
as his parents are away for the weekend.
He's done as Bram told him—
informed the neighbors
he's having a small gathering,
assured them the music won't be too loud,
promised that everyone will leave by midnight.

Even if they do complain later,
there will be no evidence of a party,
not even debris in the vacuum cleaner.
Chris's parents will feel relieved
he took such good care of the house,
he'll get off with nothing worse
than a mild reprimand.

So Bram says.

impeccable

Bram's planning is impeccable.
His "before" photos
capture a house precisely.
The placement of ornaments,
the slant of a rug,
even the contents of the fridge
are noted and photographed,
so by the end of the party
everything can be put back in place.
He gloats
that prideful householders
have no idea
their beloved home
has been at his mercy.

GABE ~ alluring

Bram's sought out guys
who are magicians
at mood lighting,
wizards at spinning just the right tunes.
He takes an empty room,
and transforms it into an alluring place
where the beat enters your bloodstream,
and softly colored lights
stroke faces and bodies.

Al says it's like a dream,
a good dream.

GABE ~ hard glitter

The sun's making my head throb.
I hate pools.
That hard glitter of water,
choking smell of chlorine,
workaholic swimmers toiling up and down,
kids shouting, dive-bombing,
sneakily pissing in the water,
radios blaring,
mums and dads with little kids
hogging the picnic tables and the shade,
the stink of stale fat from the cafeteria,
and planes screaming overhead
every sixty seconds,
just about blasting everyone out of the water.

I descend another flight of steps,
reach the grass,
and throw myself onto my towel.
Nearby is a weary-looking woman,
and a slender girl, about fifteen,
with a baby, milky-white.
The girl looks fed-up,
and so does the baby.
It has a large, lolling head and flattened face.
Amazing how alien small babies look.
And there—excellent!—high on the grassy bank
is a group of four girls,
without guys.
I'm just about to pounce,

when the baby wails.
The girl swears,
and shoves a bottle in the kid's mouth.
It squirms, kicking froggy legs,
and yells louder.
"You little shit!" hisses the girl.
The venom in her voice
makes me freeze.
I imagine what I would do
if someone spoke like that
to this little girl I know, Baby Boboli.
I'd probably kill them.
The girl doesn't see me watching,
but the woman does.
Embarrassed, she reaches over for the baby
and rocks it.
The girl snatches up her swimming cap,
springs to her feet,
and dashes away.

I gaze back at the four girls,
catch the eye of the dark-haired one,
and wave an unlit cigarette at her.
She nods, smiling shyly.
I give them the usual enticing spiel—
the party'll be smart, exclusive,
with good music, great guys,
no parents, no problems.

below the surface

Gabe dives into the water
and collides
with the girl,
the one with the baby.
"Sorry," he splutters
and offers her his beguiling grin.
She ignores him,
her face set,
and torpedoes away.
She swims as if she is alone
in the pool,
in the world,
and wants nothing to do with anyone.
Not Gabe.
And especially not that baby.

m e r m a i d

As a boy
Gabe loved the story
of how his dad and mother first met.
At a summer festival
she was down by the harbor,
arranged on a rock,
gazing out to sea.
Such a parched-looking mermaid!
Pale, dry skin, sun-bleached hair,
fishtail rustling
like autumn leaves.

"I circled her,
tried to make her smile,
but she didn't blink an eyelid.
I hung around for hours,
until at last she slipped off her tail,
and I offered to buy her a drink.
She was the thirstiest person I've ever met!
That day, on the seventh glass,
I asked her to marry me,
and I kept on asking
until she said yes."

Now that Gabe is older,
he thinks,
What an idiot!

A thirsty little mermaid
and a builder on dry land—
how on earth
could that ever have worked?

sheer poetry

Gabe's dad
has a crookback and a missing finger.
He doesn't seem
a very romantic figure
in his stained overalls and work boots.
But, even after all these years,
he's still entranced
by the poetry
of the building trade:
adobe
ashlar
birdsmouth
buttress
camber
cantilever
mandrel
mezzanine
sarking
screeding
shimming
High on a roof,
tool belt on his hips,
he chants these words,
sings them,
sends them floating on the wind.

GABE ~ fish wife

My dad has a knack
for meeting and marrying
the most bizarre women.
First my mother,
the mermaid.
Then Sara.
She works at the university
as an ichthyologist,
specializing in eels.
You'd expect her to be slimy and slippery,
but she's so warm and rosy
I understand why my dad nearly fell
off the roof
when she first smiled at him.

I like Sara,
a lot,
but she's not my mother.

GABE ~ beloved boy

My little brother, Luke,
is seven years old.
My father and Sara's beloved boy.

Luke knows the difference between
a soil pipe
a waste pipe
a vent pipe.

Luke's favorite things are
a screwdriver
a plunger
a pipe wrench.

Luke's saving up for
a closet auger
a smooth-jaw wrench
slip-joint pliers.

Luke loves
a leaking tap
a stopped-up toilet
a backed-up kitchen sink.
His dream is to unblock a sewer.
He is severely disturbed.

GABE ~ best friend

My best friend, Al,
(short for Alan and Alcohol)
complains I've got the glamorous job,
but I get bored with hanging out
at the pool
and the cinemas
and the video stores,
making small talk,
charming strangers.
Sometimes I think I'd rather
be on the clean-up crew,
then I remember those vomit-streaked toilets.
Worse, some slobs even throw up in the bath.
Ever tried scraping pizza crust
out of the drain?

Al gets drunk most nights.
He's even come drunk to school
and been suspended heaps of times.
He says he hates his life,
hates everything.

I've known him since kindergarten.
He used to be eager,
into everything,
always asking questions.
Now he's chaotic,
blurred at the edges,
drifting about in his smelly old coat.

dirty old dog

Al doesn't shower, doesn't wash.
His feet reek, his sneakers reek.
He doesn't care.

The girls in his class complain
he smells like a dirty old dog.
They won't sit near him,
they hold their noses.
Al laughs.
He doesn't care.

GABE ~ school

Most schools these days
claim to be a center of excellence
for something—English, science,
even sports.
Not Johnstone High.
Those who don't go there
slag it off as a school for losers,
and they're probably right.
But I don't mind it too much.
The teachers are friendly,
and the principal's not strict
about uniforms and that sort of stuff.
Just as well.
Bram's the only one
who wears leather shoes,
the school tie,
even a blazer.

Bram likes to stand out from the rabble.
He's a brain,
and has already mapped out his life.
Sydney University next year,
law degree,
politics.
He's going to be powerful.
Some of the kids
(and even the teachers)
find him intimidating.

death and destruction

Bram likes his name—
it means "raven,"
a bird that represents
death and destruction.

too late, mate

Chris tears at his fingernails,
worrying about the party.
He calls around,
trying to cancel,
trying to get hold of Bram or Gabe,
but everyone just says,
"Too late, mate. We're coming."
He might draw the curtains,
pretend to be out,
but Al will bang on the door,
and create such a scene
the neighbors'll probably call the cops.
Nearly doubled-over from stomachache,
he opens the door
before Bram even knocks.

GABE ~ preparations

Al and I bump past Chris,
lugging empty cardboard boxes.
Bram strolls in after us,
satanic in black,
a Polaroid camera slung
around his neck.
He acknowledges Chris's nervous smile
with a nod, and says,
"Right, mate, give us the guided tour."

There's lots of good stuff:
Persian rugs,
paintings,
an antique mirror over the mantelpiece,
a small French clock,
silver candlesticks.
Bram slips the cover off the camera.
"The usual routine:
photos first,
then pack up everything
and stash it in the master bedroom."
Chris plucks at his elbow.
"I don't think this is a good idea,"
he bleats.
"I promised my parents
I'd look after the house."
Bram brushes him away,
concentrates on wide angles,
then close-ups.

Chris looks to Al and me, appealing.
"My parents'll kill me.
I'll be grounded forever!"
Al sniggers.
"Can't ground you if you're dead."
He drifts off to the kitchen.
"Got any grog?"
Bram's head jerks up.
"Don't touch anything! You know the deal."
Al sniggers again.
"They're not going to miss one little beer,
are they?"
"Al!"
"Okay, *Boss.*"
Al sprawls in a chair, sulky.
Bram glares at me.
I know what he's thinking—
"Al is more *your* friend than mine.
If you can't control him,
he's out of the parties.
Got it?"

power

For the past few years,
Bram has felt his power
grow.

He is a force
to be unleashed.

GABE ∼ the girl of your dreams

"Please," says Chris.
"I've changed my mind."
I sigh inwardly,
make my voice kind.
"It'll be all right.
No one's going to trash the house.
Your folks won't find out."
"But . . ."
"Trust me," I say.
"Tonight you'll meet the girl of your dreams."
"I wish," Chris mutters,
unconvinced.
I can read his mind—
It's not fair everyone falls for Gabe,
just because he's good-looking.
He treats them like dirt, too.
One-night stands, nothing more.
If I had a girl, I'd love her.

I turn away.
Yeah, yeah, yeah.
He doesn't know I hate it
that girls marvel at my face,
but never want to see me,
real me.

triumph

When the party's well underway
Gabe takes his latest girl, Natalie,
into the garden.
The air is sweet with jasmine.
She strokes the back of his neck,
nibbles his ear.
Her teeth are small, white, perfect.
He pulls away.
"Look, I don't think this is going to work."
She sucks in her breath,
disbelieving.
"You're dumping me?"
Gabe can tell this is a first for her.
"Yup."
She springs up.
There is rage, but no grief, in her eyes.
"You shit!"
She slaps him, hard.

Gabe watches her storm away,
his small feeling of triumph dissipating.
He waits,
then goes back to the party.

There are three possibilities—
Anna, Jo, Emma.
They're all beautiful, cold-eyed.
Any one of them will do.

the ambush

Gabe crouches on the stairs,
concealed by railings long as grass.
He stares down at the party,
eyes and ears alert,
body tightly coiled.
He is preparing to spring,
preparing to strike.

fucked up

They're so different,
Gabe and Bram and Al,
they don't know why or how
they became friends.
After a Personal Development unit,
Brain says knowingly,
"Because we're all fucked-up in some way."
"So how do we get unfucked?" asks Gabe.
"Fucked if I know," says Bram.
"Fucked if I care," says Al.
"Hey," says a passing teacher,
"watch that language, you lot!"
"Sure," says Al. "Fuckin' sorry, sir."
He gets an afternoon detention,
shrugs,
"What the fuck."

failing

Al is failing every subject.
His teachers are concerned,
then impatient—
"Look at me when I'm speaking to you!"
But Al looks no one in the eye.
Even his friends have forgotten
that his eyes are as shiny as river stones.

an unkindness of ravens

The group names for birds
can be beautiful:
a bouquet of pheasants
a charm of finches
a skein of geese
a company of parrots
a paddling of ducks
a murmuration of starlings
an exaltation of larks.
But there is also
a murder of crows
an unkindness of ravens.

Ravens are the largest members
of the crow family—
solitary
sharp
sinister.
In certain lights
their black feathers shine
metallic purple, violet.
Sometimes when Bram catches a glimpse
of his dark hair,
he sees the same sheen,
and he smiles.

caravan park

Bram lives in a caravan park
with his mother and two sisters.
It's cheaper than renting a flat.
The little girls cut pictures
out of magazines,
and pretend they live in a fairy-tale palace.
But Bram can't escape from
the mean line of vans,
the rotting picnic tables,
the flies in summer,
the mud in winter.

He catches two buses to school,
and never brings friends home.

On Sundays he does the family washing
in the dank communal laundry,
hangs it up, watches it dry.
They can't risk its being stolen.

hate

Bram hates his father.
Hates him for gambling away
the house, the money.
Hates him for dying drunk
under the wheels of a 420 bus.
Hates him for leaving
a sick wife and three children
penniless
friendless
powerless.

houses

Bram loves the houses,
hates the houses.
Hates their closed doors,
hates their glowing windows,
hates seeing them
smug with families,
hearing them breathe,
"Keep out. Keep out."

Bram loves the houses,
hates the houses.
Loves them
when they are his for the taking,
to be treasured, or trashed.
Loves them
stripped bare,
vulnerable.

He knows
the other partygoers think
he's strange,
not drinking, eating, dancing.
Just watching from the shadows.

They don't know
his secret gratification.

GABE ~ silly bugger

The music's low and slow.
I stare deep into Anna's eyes.
She stares back
like a mesmerized rabbit.
I want to laugh.

"Hey, Gabe! Catch!"
Al is on the stairs, swaying,
his eyes dazed.
In his hands is something
small,
round as a head.
He throws.
It soars across the room,
smashes into the wall
with a soft, sick thud.
Pulp, pips, juice.
A melon.
Al, you silly bugger.
Bram knifes through the crowd,
bounds up the stairs,
grabs a fistful of Al's hair,
drags him.
He grinds Al's face
into the orange mush.
"Clean it up!
Then get out!"
Al looks around, humiliated,
his face smeared like a little kid's.

I abandon the rabbit,
and silently help him
scrape up the mess,
scrub down the wall.

the coat

Al shuffles down the road
in an old army coat so big
it drags on the ground.
The sleeves are so long
it seems he has no hands.

He wears the coat,
summer and winter.
Without it he would be
a snail without its shell—
soft
exposed
defenseless.

indifference

Al doesn't know
when his parents stopped
loving each other.
It happened insidiously,
like damp creeping up a wall.
Now the damage is so extensive
there's no remedy
but to pull the structure down
and start again.

He wishes they would
argue, shout, smash.
Anything would be better
than the silence
of indifference.

the celebration

At a party—
some big family celebration—
Gabe's mother told him
she was leaving.
They were in the shadowy back garden,
away from the light and laughter
spilling out of the house.
Her voice was sorrowful, confiding,
as if talking to a grown man.
She was very drunk,
already an outsider
among this tribe, her husband's people.

Gabe shifted in her grasp,
wanting to escape her sour breath,
but, at the same time,
wanting to hold on to her.
Then his father,
face contorted with anger and grief,
picked him up,
although he was a big seven-year-old,
and whisked him into the house,
murmuring, "It's going to be all right, son."
Over his father's shoulder,
Gabe saw his mother bury her face
in her hands,
her long, glittering skirt curved
around her legs
like a mermaid's tail.

In the morning, Gabe tramped
through the garden,
ripping bedraggled party streamers,
crushing empty beer cans,
knocking over abandoned wineglasses.
His chest hurting.

don't go

"Don't go," he begged.
"Take me with you," he pleaded.
But, with scarcely a splash,
his mother sailed away
with her lover
on a yacht as big as a palace.
He hated her then,
his pale, parched mother.

As he grew older
and saw *her* face looking back at him
from the mirror,
he hated
his own face, too.

pallor

Gabe is rarely ill—
yet people are struck
by the pallor of his skin.
It's as if his blood
has been diverted
to the core of his body
in a desperate attempt
to keep it warm.

GABE ~ the box

I keep my mother
in a box
under my bed.
Well, not my mother, exactly,
but all the letters
she has written to me
over the years.
Unopened.

GABE ~ junk, not treasure

One rainy afternoon,
Luke runs out of pipes,
goes scrounging
around the house
for cardboard tubes.
He sticks his sharp little nose
under my bed,
finds the box of letters.

I hear him squealing
with surprise,
catch him handling the letters
as if they were treasure.

I pick him up
by the back of his shirt,
toss him out of my room.
"Keep out! Stay out!"
He stares at me
with big, bewildered eyes.
I slam the door shut,
kick the box back under the bed.

GABE ~ on the walls

Girls phone me
all the time.
I never bring them home.
It was a puzzle to Dad and Sara
until the parent-teacher interviews.

After they'd endured three hours
of teachers telling them
I was underachieving,
Sara bolted into the girls' toilets.
And, there,
scrawled all over the walls, was
"Gabe Fellows is a shit."
"Gabe screws around."
"I've been dumped by Gabe Fellows."
"So what? Who hasn't?"

Mortified.
Sara sat there
with her pants around her ankles,
unable to believe she was reading
these things about her son.
"*Step*son," I corrected her.
That cut her, and I was sorry,
but it stopped her from ranting on.
Then my dad tried to talk man-to-man,
but I yelled at him
to mind his own business,
and barged out of the room.

beautiful but heartless

Sara says to Gabe,
"You are in danger of becoming
a beautiful but heartless man."

She speaks softly, with such regret,
it takes Gabe a while to realize
just what she's said.
He boots one of Luke's pipes
across the room.
"And you're an ugly, boring eel-woman!"

GABE ~ rotten to the core

My father insists on showing me
an old house he's restoring.
"It has lovely bones," he says.
Yeah, gorgeous.
"I've got masses of homework,"
I remind him.
He leads me to the kitchen.
It smells musty.
"Stamp on the floor," he says.
The old man's going mad,
but I stamp.
The wood's soft and mushy.
My foot disappears
into a splintery black hole.
"Thanks, Dad."
He looks at me, long and slow.
"When something's rotten,
you have to rip it out.
Otherwise it'll spread,
causing serious damage and decay."

I know he's not talking about floorboards.

sara

Sara finds Gabe watching
a late-night program
about Afghani children.
They are starving,
their eyes huge,
uncomprehending,
their shoulder blades
like wire coat hangers.
Gabe's so shaken
he can hardly speak.
Sara sits next to him,
keeps him company
to the bitter end,
taken aback
by the tender beating of his heart.

baby boboli

Gabe has a secret—
he is besotted with
the baby daughter of
Christina and Gino Boboli,
who run the corner shop.

When their daughter is born,
Christina and Gino can't agree
on a name.
By the time they decide on Isabella,
it's too late—
the customers know her as
Baby Boboli.

When Gabe first sees her,
she's being weighed in the scales
like prize potatoes.
Gabe laughs,
she wrinkles her nose,
and the two of them fall in love.

a great father

Christina sees how girls flutter
when Gabe comes into the shop.
She sees his carelessness,
his contempt.
Yet he's gentle
with her little daughter.
She tells him,
"You'll make a great father, one day!"
Gabe snorts.
"No chance!
I'm never getting married."
Gino overhears.
"Good on yer, mate," he says.
"Women aren't worth the trouble."
Christina throws an orange at him,
he ducks, laughing.
Gabe smiles,
but Christina and Gino make him feel
lonely.

the children's playground

Gabe takes Baby Boboli
to the children's playground in the park.
She's captivated
by the yellow boat in the sandpit.
"Rock it!" she orders. *"Please!"*
Gabe joggles the boat,
she proudly steers
through crashing waves,
past sharks and crocodiles and whales.
"Sing!" she commands. *"Please!"*
And Gabe obediently chants,
"Row, row, row your boat . . ."
The tune catches in his head,
and he finds himself humming it at school,
much to Al and Bram's derision.

u n c l e

As well as Christina and Gino
at the corner shop,
there is Uncle.
Wispy
and deaf,
he drifts like a silent ghost,
unpacking goods,
shifting boxes of vegetables.
Christina and Gino
conjure up jobs
to make him feel useful.
Uncle never smiles,
and when he's hanging bunches of onions
from the stout beam in the shop
he thinks of the rope coiled
at the bottom of his cupboard.

Baby Boboli saves his life.
It's his task to look after her,
feed her,
play with her.
They sit on a chair outside the shop,
leafing through picture books,
and when it's stinking hot,
she splashes in a plastic paddling pool
in the middle of the pavement.
Baby Boboli loves
her mum and dad,

and all the customers,
especially Gabe,
who waggles his ears
to make her laugh,
but most of all,
she loves Uncle.

GABE ~ signing

I spoke to Uncle once,
in sign language.
I just said, "Hello."
His eyes widened,
and his face creased
into the biggest smile I've ever seen.
He started signing at top speed,
words flowing
from his fingertips
and I had to say,
"Whoa, sorry!"

Christina is ashamed
she and Gino never learned
to sign more than a few basic words.
They've never had a proper conversation
with Uncle.
So I got a book out of the library,
and now I'm learning
ten new signs a day.
Every time I go to the shop,
I teach Baby Boboli what I know.
One day she and Uncle will talk
nonstop.

holes

On Sunday,
Gabe treats Luke to the movies,
but the little boy is more entranced
by the holes all over the city.
He stops at each excavation,
peering curiously through the fences.
He is awed by
the giant drainage pipes.
"They're so big you could live in them!"
Gabe laughs—
he can just see Luke as a little old man
making a pipe his home!

On the bus,
Luke chatters on about holes
but Gabe stares out of the window.
He feels tired and empty,
as if his chest is a great abandoned hole,
encased by rusty scaffolding.

GABE ～ demons

Luke's fascination with drainage
extends to waterspouts—
those grotesque stone gargoyles
jeering from rooftops.

He and Dad tramp through the city
searching out fantastic creatures
clinging to edges and ledges.
Luke loves the idea
of water gushing, rushing
out of their mouths.
Dad hasn't the heart to tell him
many of these creatures
have outlived their usefulness,
their mouths are now
plugged
with concrete.

Luke shows me
a book of ancient gargoyles.
Some are demonic—
mad eyes,
screaming mouths—
far too scary for a kid.
Luke studies them, unblinking,
but they make me shudder.
When I close my eyes
it's as if I'm inside a gargoyle,
looking out.

passions

Gabe's interests never last long—
his bedroom is a graveyard
of fleeting passions:
baseball, trumpet,
astronomy, photography,
rock-climbing, skateboarding . . .
Sara grumbles,
"I wish you'd stick to something."
Gabe shrugs.
"Why are *you* so obsessed with eels?"
She smiles, remembering,
and tells Gabe about the day
her father took her fishing at the Parramatta River.
"He said the word *Parramatta* means
'Where eels lie down.'
I imagined the riverbed all ribbony
with drowsing eels.
I started reading about them, and I liked them.
The young ones—the elvers—
are determined little critters.
They'll even clamber up
slippery dam walls
to get where they want to go."

Determination.
That's another thing that mystifies Gabe.
He knows if he was an eel
he'd be the one left behind in the dam
as the others sought a route to the river.

drifting

Sara tells Gabe
how the larvae of eels
drift
across vast seas
to find a place
where they have never been.

Somehow the larvae know
where they are heading,
whereas Gabe feels he may drift
on and on,
past shore
after shore
after shore.

GABE ~ the trade

Don't know much
about mermaids.
Just the story of
the little mermaid
who fell in love with a mortal,
and traded
her voice for legs.

I wonder if my mother is happy
with her trade?

GABE ~ fish

Luke doesn't share
Sara's passion for eels.
The only fish
that interests him
is—surprise, surprise—
the pipefish!
Perhaps the kid's
not so seriously disturbed after all.

bram's ravens

In Norse mythology,
the god Odin had two ravens,
Thought and Memory.
He sent them into the world
to discover
the ways and deeds of man.

Two black ravens are stalking Bram.
He sees them
at the caravan park,
at school,
outside the shopping center.
He starts carrying bread
in his pockets,
scatters crumbs as he walks.
With grim self-knowing
he names them
Malice and Envy.
One day the ravens
will perch on his shoulders,
and he'll send them out
into the world
to feed
and fatten.

brief encounter

Al truants from school,
mooches around the city.
Outside the station,
a woman asks him for a light.
They smoke, get talking.
Her name is Leanne.
She travels the trains at night;
it's easier than looking for lodging.
She sleeps during the day;
much safer that way.
Besides, she likes a bed of grass,
a ceiling of clouds and brilliant blue sky.

It almost sounds romantic,
but she's smelly,
and her hair is matted like
a sick dog's.
Before she stumbles away,
she slips some money
into the top pocket of Al's coat.
"Get a bed for the night," she advises.
Al's face burns.
"*She* thinks *I'm* a bum!"

GABE ~ until morning

Party time again.
Another house,
another gaggle of girls.

Someone called Helen
asks me to dance.
She has a damaged face,
but her smile is electrifying!
When I've picked myself up off the floor,
we find a quiet place to sit and talk.
And talk.
And talk.

We are easy, comfortable,
as if we've known each other
all our lives.
I tell her about my dad and Sara and Luke.
I tell her about my mermaid mother.
About the night of that long-ago party.
About the letters under my bed.

She wraps her arms around me,
and stays
until morning.

GABE ~ something malevolent

I dream
something malevolent
is crouching on my chest.
I feel my lungs crushing, bubbling.
My throat burns.
I scream inside my head—
and wake with a jolt.
I lie, eyes staring, thinking,
What the fuck was that?

GABE ~ no calls

There are so many girls,
I don't remember
their faces, their names.
Sara gets fed up
taking messages,
lying for me,
saying I'm out.
She yells now from the kitchen,
"Gabe! Phone!"
"Who is it?" I call back.
"She says her name's Helen—
and it's urgent."
"Don't know any Helen."
"She says to tell you Helen of Gordon."
Ah.
That girl.
She twisted my heart.
She saw into my soul.
I shout,
"Tell her I've left the country!"

HELEN

HELEN ~ circus freak

I am Helen,
and I was born with the face of a pig.
In a previous age
I'd have been a circus freak.
People would have paid good money
to roll up, roll up,
come and gawp,
come and gasp,
come and thrill with horror
at The Ugliest Girl in the World!

Luckily, I was born in the 20th century
to parents who could pay good money
to doctors and plastic surgeons.
I still look a bit piggy,
no one's ever going to offer me
a modeling contract,
but I can walk down the street now
without turning heads.
Bliss.

HELEN ~ just a load of orifices

The human face
is just a load of orifices:
nose-hole for breathing
mouth-hole for eating
eye-holes for seeing
ear-holes for hearing.
Imagine if there was no
bone
or muscle
or cartilage
or pearly skin
to embellish them.

HELEN ~ little sister

Mum and Dad waited a long time—
seven years, to be precise—
before they risked having another child.
Can you blame them?
They didn't want
two piggywigs in the family.

My sister, Celeste, was born normal.
(Phew!)
And *beautiful*.

I used to stare at her for ages.
My parents would find me by her cot,
my face pressed against the railings.
They'd shoo me out of the room.
I realize now they were afraid
I would hurt Celeste,
but I was just trying to work out
what made her so lovable,
and me not.

HELEN ~ celestial

My father is
dull,
solid.
I can't think why he chose
the name Celeste.
It means "heavenly."

Perhaps after the Hell of me,
he was elated
to have fathered
such a divine being.

HELEN ~ let's face it

When I was growing up,
my face, my ears, my neck,
my whole body
would burn,
and I would stare hard at nothing
when I heard
these phrases:
face to face
on the face of it
two-faced
face about
facedown
face-lift
face it out
face the music
fly in the face of
save face
take it at face value
off your face
shut your face
not just a pretty face!

HELEN ∼ stay at home

My mother doesn't go to work.
Dad believes
women should be at home,
looking after the family.
He lets her do volunteer work
at the hospital,
provided it's during school hours
and doesn't interfere
with the running of the house.
She gardens,
arranges flowers,
dishes up banquets
for my father's business associates.
I've started watching her like a hawk
to see if that fixed smile ever slips,
but it doesn't.

My life will be different.
I will be an excellent plastic surgeon,
specializing in deformities.
And *if* I marry,
it will *not* be to a bossy, bossy man.

the volunteer

Every day
Helen's mother goes
to the children's hospital
to hold a drowned child
in her arms.
She does it because
the parents are exhausted.
She does it because she is grateful
this is not her child.
She does it because the beating
of her heart against his
might one day wake him up.
His body is as light as a bouquet of flowers.
His head rests on her shoulder
as fragile as thistledown.

She doesn't tell her family
what she does at the hospital,
and they don't ask.
They probably think
she dispenses drinks,
plays games,
sings songs.

She does sing.
She sings softly into the child's ear,
sings of all the good things waiting for him.
Singing, hoping he is dreaming,
hoping to lure him back to the world.

HELEN ~ a man of habit

My dad is a man of appalling regularity.
He gets up at six,
leaves for work at seven,
comes home at eight,
goes to bed at eleven.

On Saturdays he plays golf at ten,
mows the lawn at three,
reads the papers from four to six.

He has sex (with my mother)
once a week,
Sundays at nine.
Gruesome, but true.

I'm scared I'll develop
his Susceptibility to Habit,
so I don't use an alarm clock,
or wear a watch.
I dye my hair black,
or streak it blond.
I walk five different ways to school.
And when my father complains,
"You're so unpredictable, Helen!"
I respond with
a smirk,
or a scowl,
or a growl.

clash

From the time Helen is no taller
than a doll's stroller,
she and her father wrangle.
"Why should I?" she asks.
"Just do as I say."
"But you're wrong!" she argues.
"Don't talk back to me!"

They impale each other
with their eyes.
She sees anger and contempt.
He sees frustration and rage.
He's used to managing 200 employees,
but
this child
this girl
this young woman
is impossibly unruly.

HELEN ~ my father speaks

My father speaks.
My mother nods.
My father lectures.
My mother nods.
My father criticizes.
My mother nods.
Imagine if
she dared to disagree,
dared to shake her head
and say *no*.
Before that happens,
trees would walk!
Birds would talk!

a tough little bird

Helen's mother grew up
in Tasmania,
where a flightless bird,
the native hen,
dives into flowing water
and strides along the riverbed,
against the current.

Ever since she was little,
Helen's mother has called her "Hen."
It's a private name for when
they're alone.
She says it softly, affectionately.
"You're a tough little bird, Hen.
Never forget that."

x-ray vision

Helen's deformity
has honed her sensitivity.
She sees through
people,
bullshit,
facades,
flimsy and false
as old buildings
that have had their insides
ripped out.
She sees through
skin and flesh and bone
into the heart
of others,
into hidden desires.

But she has a blind spot
when it comes to her parents.
It's like a floater in the eye,
obscuring vision.

HELEN ∼ something to praise

When you're not pretty
people seize on something to praise—
your friendly eyes,
your shining hair,
your shell-like ears.
In my case it's my smile—
not the one I was born with, of course,
that was barely human.
This smile is man-made,
but now it's all mine!

HELEN ~ transformation

The human face
has forty-four muscles.
You use twenty to smile,
forty to frown.
I love their names:
frontalis
nasalis
occipitalis
platysma
masseter
splenius capitis
orbicularis oculis.
One day I will
sculpt bone,
repair muscle,
graft skin.
I will transform
the deformed.

HELEN ~ not a party girl

I'm not the most
popular girl in the school,
but I'm invited to a lot of parties.
Other girls feel comfortable around me.
They believe they look better than me.
They believe they'll always have me
to talk to when everyone else
is drifting off with partners.
How dare they judge me!
How stupid to put beauty above all else!
I refuse to be used.

planning

Helen's best friend, Barb,
is set on going to a party
on the other side of the city.
It involves planning
and lies to parents.
Reluctantly, Helen agrees.
"But I'm not staying late,"
she warns. "Okay?"
"Okay," says Barb,
face angelic,
fingers crossed.

party time

Helen and Barb
live north of the city
in houses as big as castles,
marooned by lawns,
screened by trees and hedges.
Neighbors wave to each other from cars,
no one pops in for a chat,
except at Christmas
when they exchange shortbreads.

On Saturday evening,
they venture across the bridge,
into unfamiliar territory.
Their parents believe
they are staying overnight
at a classmate's,
but they are going to a party,
invited by a friend of a friend of a friend.

the boys

Through a haze
of cigarette smoke,
Helen observes the boys.
She sees Bram,
watchful as a bird of prey,
Al sunk in a corner,
joylessly swigging from a bottle,
but it is Gabe
who takes her breath away—
where his heart should be
is a deep, dark hollow.
Dizzily, she grabs the edge of a table,
shuts her eyes.
When she looks again,
all she sees is the boy's
crumpled shirt,
but she knows
the hollow exists.

HELEN ~ so what's your name?

Barb is flamboyant,
dancing wildly on her own.
All the boys are watching her,
including Gabe.
He hasn't noticed me,
though I stand right next to him.
I know he'll never ask me to dance,
so I ask him.
"Sure," he says, his eyes still on Barb.
It's almost a whole song later,
when we're swaying to the music,
my head resting on his shoulder,
that he says,
"So what's your name?"
"Helen."
"Helen of Troy whose face
launched a thousand ships?"
The question is mechanical;
he's used this line before.
"No," I say,
"Helen of Gordon whose face
wrecked a thousand ships."
He stops dancing,
tilts up my chin,
and looks at me
for the first time.

HELEN ～ staying on

I check that Barb's got a lift
to her friend's place,
and tell her that Gabe and I
are staying on for a while.
She flounces off,
taken aback—and envious!

leap

Helen has never been
with a boy before.
She doesn't know why
she has a feeling of rightness
about this one,
especially as that desolate void
in his chest
makes him so dangerous.

She leaps right in.

HELEN ~ revelations

We tell each other things,
things we've never told anyone.
We gaze at each other in awe,
then all is quiet, all is lovely.

HELEN ~ good looks

"Don't blame you.
He's stunning-looking,"
says Barb the next day.
"Is he? I hadn't noticed."
Barb gives a skeptical snort.
But it's true.
I'd mainly been struck
by the paleness of his skin,
as if he never sees the sun,
and by the longing
with which he held me.

HELEN ~ waiting

I wait.
He doesn't call.
Perhaps he's lost my phone number.
Perhaps he's forgotten my surname.
I wait.
I wait and wait.
I phone him.
He's not there.
He's never there.
I leave my name and number
with his father,
with Sara,
with Luke.
I wait and wait.
He doesn't call.

HELEN

Fuck him.

HELEN ~ a drop of blood

Every morning I wake,
desperate to see
a drop of blood.
I rush to the toilet,
several times a day,
hoping this time, this time.
Please, please, please!
I've always found my period
a pain.
Now all I want
is to flood with blood.

HELEN ~ prayers

"Didn't you use a condom?"
Barb is shocked.
"Of course!"
"Jeez . . . what're you going to do?"
I bite my lip,
don't answer.
What *am* I going to do?

I don't believe in God.
I don't want to believe in someone
who lets freaks be born,
who doesn't stop
all the misery and suffering
in the world.

Despising myself,
I pray.

HELEN ~ confirmation

Barb comes with me
to the doctor's.
She flips through
old *Who* magazines
while I find out
what I already know.
My mouth is so dry
I can hardly speak.

The doctor assures me
this conversation is confidential,
but she wants me
to tell my parents
immediately.
"You have options," she says.
She is sympathetic,
but weary.
I can tell she is thinking,
Don't these kids know
about contraception?

HELEN ～ messages

I call Gabe.
I leave messages.
It's Helen.
It's urgent.
He doesn't call back.

I try again.
In the background
I hear his shouting voice,
"Tell her I've left the country!"
His stepmother, Sara, says,
"I'm very sorry."

HELEN ～ someone, my one

An abortion.
It's probably the sensible thing
to do, to do, to do.
But I have someone growing inside me,
someone who will think and feel, laugh and cry.
Can I let them dig out this someone, my one?
Can I let them discard this someone, my one?
It's probably the sensible thing
to do, to do, to do.
I stroke my stomach,
stroke and soothe
my one, my one, my one.

I'm pregnant

One night,
Helen tells her parents
"I'm pregnant."
The room, the house, the world
is quiet
as if the inhabitants have fled.
Her mother whispers,
"Oh, Helen, are you sure?"
Her father says,
"You stupid little bitch!"

She sits stony-faced,
as the questions,
the recriminations,
strike her like waves
crashing against a cliff.

She won't tell them who the father is.
Not that it matters.
"You'll have it aborted, of course,"
states her father.
"No."
She looks appealingly at her mother.
She needs her to say,
"What do *you* want to do, Helen?
Whatever it is, I'll help."

But her mother is silent.

HELEN ~ moving out

I throw clothes in a bag
and go to stay with Barb.
Her parents are kind, polite,
but I know they won't want me
around for long.

I curl up on a trundle bed
in Barb's room.
We eat chips
and play music
and chatter into the night.
We're little kids again,
having a sleepover,
but in the morning
my parents won't be coming
to pick me up.
I won't be going home.

HELEN ~ journey

One Sunday morning
I stand across the road
from Gabe's house.
It's a tall terrace, sunflower yellow,
with green latticework.
I like the rambling shrubs
in the small front garden.
My heart is beating so violently
it's about to jump out
of my chest.
I force my shaking legs to move.
Only twenty steps,
but it feels like a journey
to the end of the earth.

As I reach for the gate,
the front door opens,
and a woman—Sara?—appears,
holding a pair of gardening gloves and clippers.
She smiles at me. "Hello?"
I swallow,
croak, "Hi, is Gabe home?"
She shakes her head.
"Nope. Not back from a party last night."
We stare at each other.
I can feel her warmth and sympathy.
This is not the first time
a nervous girl has turned up
on the doorstep.

"Can I help?" she asks.
The words
I'd wanted from my mother.

I turn,
plunge down the street.

HELEN ~ dropping out

I need a job.
I need somewhere to live.
I need to get my life together,
so I drop out of school.

The school counselor says,
"Think carefully about this.
You're throwing away a brilliant career.
You could be anything you want to be."
I tell her, "I'll still do it, one day."
She shakes her head.
"You have no idea how hard it is
bringing up a child on your own."
But I do.
I've read books.
I've seen movies.
I push back my chair.
I'll manage.

I'm terrified.

HELEN ~ the dish pig

I walk the streets,
searching for a job.
The supermarkets take my name,
don't ring back.
I apply at gas stations,
dress shops,
drugstores,
restaurants.
They all want experience.
Finally, I'm offered a job at a café
as a dish pig.
When I wince,
thinking the chef is making fun of my face,
he says impatiently,
"Kitchen-hand, you know—dish pig."

He shows me the kitchen.
Tiny and as hot as a sauna.
There are buckets,
stacks of dirty plates,
four sinks,
one dishwasher,
and a young man—Filipino, I think—
scouring a pot as big as a bath.
His skin is slick with sweat.
"This is Tony," says the chef.
The young man gives a funny little bow.
"I would say," he says,
"it is a pleasure to meet you."

The chef digs wax out of his ear.
"So," he says, "want the job?"
Tony blinks at me, his face hopeful.
"I do."

HELEN ~ my brilliant career

In the steamy, dingy kitchen,
this is my brilliant career—
I soak cutlery in buckets
of warm, soapy water.
I scrub greasy pots,
scrape plates,
rinse them,
load them into the dishwasher.
When the plates are dry,
I put them away,
and load the next lot.

I also
peel and slice vegetables,
chop chunks of meat,
pull off prawn heads and tails.
I stink of fish.

I wipe down tables,
stack chairs,
mop floors,
and dump the garbage in the alley.
Cockroaches as big as security guards
lounge about the bins.

Tony and I are always the last to leave.

HELEN ~ waiting empty

My arms ache,
my back aches,
my legs ache,
my feet ache.

I droop over the sink,
tears leaking out of my eyes.
Tony pats me on the shoulder,
and makes a cup of black coffee.

I let it all spill out—
Gabe,
the baby,
needing somewhere to live.

Tony's face brightens
at this last bit of info.
"I would say,
I have just the place for you."

He tells me about
Mrs. Evans and her boardinghouse.
"I don't think she rents rooms
for the money.
She is lonely, perhaps.
There's me and Mr. Scroop—
such a funny old fellow!"

I wipe my face.

"And there's a spare room?"

"Yes!" says Tony.

"It has been waiting empty all this time—
just for you!"

mr. scroop

Mr. Scroop has no family,
except for a son
who owns some sort of export business.
Mr. Scroop is vague about the details.

Mr. Scroop is always rushing.
He rushes to the bank,
rushes to mail a letter,
rushes to the shops,
rushes home
in case his son
has phoned or dropped in.
In the three years he has lived
at Mrs. Evans's
he has not heard a word
from his son,
but he will not hear a word said
against him.

HELEN ~ the landlady

On the way to the boardinghouse
Tony says, "I would say,
Mrs. Evans can seem like a cross lady,
but she's very nice, I assure you."
A bead of sweat trickles down my forehead.
"Do I tell her about the baby?"
Tony looks thoughtful.
At last he says, "I would say,
you cannot lie if she asks you.
But why should she think such a thing?"

And she doesn't.
She asks me about drugs.
"No," I answer. "Never."
"Do you give me your word?"
"I do."
She purses her lips.
"I don't usually have young girls here,
but Tony has just about begged me
to death."
"He's a good friend," I say,
and that seems to decide her.
"The room's ready.
You can move in as soon as you wish."

HELEN ~ packing up

I collect my bag
from Barb's house,
then I go home.
I knock on the door
like a stranger.
No one answers,
so I let myself in.
The curtains are half-drawn,
the rooms are cool and dark.
I want to crouch in that darkness,
wrap it around me,
hide in it for ever.

Mechanically,
I pack up my things,
and tuck my old teddy bear
into Celeste's bed.
It's missing an eye,
but she's always liked it.
Then I phone for a cab,
and leave my front-door key
on the dining-room table,
next to a vase of full-blown roses.

HELEN ~ teary

The cab driver is cheery,
I am teary.
My crying makes him
very uncomfortable
so he keeps chattering.
"Did you know, there are three kinds
of tears? Basal, reflex, and emotional.
Fact.
Did you know, most animals
don't cry? Seals do, to get rid of salt.
Fact.
Did you know, there was a woman
who shed tears from her right eye
when she was thinking about her mother,
and from her left eye
when she was thinking about her father?
Fact."
I stop crying.
"Really?"
He nods.
"I listen to the radio a lot."
He helps me carry my stuff
up the steps to the house,
and refuses to take money for the fare.
"I have a daughter about your age.
Good luck."

renting out

Mrs. Evans reprimands herself
for having rented out the room
to this young girl,
when she really needs a *useful* man
who would offer to help
repair the gutters,
replace rotten wood,
fix the fence,
do a bit of painting.
This big old Federation house
is falling into disrepair.
Even the front veranda
is wrenching away,
as if it's weary of being attached
for so long.
She knows how it feels.
She measures the gap—
three fingers wide now,
and the front door is starting to jam.

But there was something
about the girl Helen . . .
Something brave about the way
she presented her damaged face
to the world,
as if to say "This is me. Handle it."
And that smile when she left!
Mrs. Evans doesn't often use the word
but the girl's smile was *ravishing*.

l e a n n e

Mrs. Evans has a granddaughter,
Leanne.
She's not a girl,
she's a woman,
nearly thirty.
She has no home,
no husband,
no child.
Just a ferocious habit.
Her parents have given up trying to help.
They've sold their house
and moved to the coast,
seeking solace in sea and sun.
No one there knows they have a daughter.
They can pretend she doesn't exist.

addiction

Mrs. Evans goes with Leanne
to a drug counseling session.
The place smells of hospital food.
While they wait, Mrs. Evans tries to read
a magazine article,
but she can't get beyond the first paragraph.
The whole session becomes a blur,
except for one thing.
The counselor says,
"If you want Leanne to give up drugs,
perhaps you need to give up
your addiction as well?"
It's such a hard thing
this woman has said
that Mrs. Evans sits, stunned.
Leanne laughs.
"She'll never give up her ciggies.
She *loves* them!"
Mrs. Evans wants to say,
"My addiction doesn't hurt anyone
except myself.
I pay my bills,
I don't lie or steal."
But, deep down, she knows
there's some truth
in what the woman has said.

The next morning
she throws her cigarettes
in the trash,
but Leanne doesn't see, doesn't know.
She has already vanished,
along with the VCR.

HELEN ~ studying

I enroll
to study by correspondence.
I can do it.
I've always
been able to do anything
I want to.
In spite of my job,
in spite of the baby,
I will pass my exams
with top marks.
I will, I will, I will.

HELEN ~ correspondence school

Fat brown envelopes
arrive almost daily—
full of notes,
instructions,
assignments,
lists of further reading.

I rip them open,
devour the contents.
Greedily,
my brain feasts.

HELEN ~ the list

I'm doing double shifts
at the café.
I can't refuse—
the owner bullies,
and, besides,
I need the money.
I've made a list
of all the things
I'll need for the baby.

Every
day
the
list
gets
longer
as
I
think
of
something
else.

I tear up the list
when I remember
list-making is one of
my father's favorite occupations.

HELEN ~ scary

Only when my stomach
starts to swell
do I truly understand.
This is *real*.
There *really* is someone
growing inside me,
someone who's going to depend
on me.
Me.

the beggar

Mrs. Evans dreams
she is lining up
at a bus stop on George Street.
A scruffy young woman
is begging.
Idly, Mrs. Evans notes
the frowsy blond hair,
the shuffling feet,
the bowed head,
as the woman silently
holds out her hand.
People shake their heads,
or look away, feeling invaded.
Only when the woman gets close
does Mrs. Evans realize . . .
"Leanne?"
Her heart lurches,
but the woman trails away,
remote as a sleepwalker,
and is lost in the crowd.

HELEN ~ getting behind

I can't keep up
with the assignments.
I can't make sense
of the math.
I stare at knotty collections
of figures.
I am stupid, stupid, stupid.
Stupid
to believe
I could work
and study.
Stupid
to believe
I could do anything
I wanted to.
Stupid, stupid, stupid.

HELEN ~ on-screen

I go to the hospital
for an ultrasound
to make sure everything's
okay with the baby.

I watch the screen,
expecting to see a blob.
But I see a baby gliding,
nearly fully formed.
It's hard to believe
this little person
is in my body.
My body!

"Do you want to know the sex?"
the doctor asks.
"Or would you like it to be a surprise?"
No more surprises.
No more of the unknown.

It is a boy!
I skip through the hospital doors,
hugging a printout of my boy.
My boy!
I'll call him Raphael.

HELEN ~ woman waiting

"There's a woman wants to see you,"
says the waiter.
I peer over the swing door
of the kitchen.
She is sitting alone at a table,
swamped
by the jumbo-sized menu.
My mother.
"I don't want to see her,"
I tell the waiter.
He shrugs,
and I turn back to the sink.
She stays for three hours,
waiting.
She doesn't order anything to eat,
just drinks coffee.
She hates coffee.

loss

For a week now
Helen's dad has been leaving
for the office as usual at seven—
then spending the day on a bench
in the park.

He's heard about men like himself—
men too ashamed to tell their families
they have lost their jobs.

When he glances at the ground,
he sees no shadow.
When he glances in a store window,
he sees no reflection.
He is ceasing to exist.

HELEN ~ belly talk

It's weird how
complete strangers
feel free
to touch my stomach,
pat it,
rub it.

It's even weirder
how they talk
to my belly.
"Hello, baby!"
"Hello in there!"
"Keeping nice and warm—
that's the way!"
I wonder if it's possible
to teach
your bump
to talk back?

HELEN ~ stalking

My mother is stalking me.
She's outside the café
when I start work,
she's even there when I finish.

"Go home," I tell her.
"Leave me alone."
But she trots after me
to the bus stop
like a stubborn old dog.
"Please, Helen. Don't be so hard.
Let me help. Let me."

She looks so defeated,
her trousers flapping around her skinny legs,
that I nearly give in.
I make my voice gruff.
"Where were you when I needed you?"
I don't wait for her answer.
I jump onto the bus
and let it carry me away.
As tears roll down my face,
I realize I'm weeping
from my right eye.
Fact.

helen's mum and dad

Theirs is the standard double bed,
but the gulf between them
is deepening, darkening.
He wakes.
She wakes.
Neither moves a muscle
in the heart-stopping blackness.

HELEN ~ birth partner

It seems I'll need
a birth partner—
someone to mop my brow,
and help me with the breathing.

I ask Barb if she'll do it.
She's thrilled,
but her parents say no.
They are pleasant to me,
but I know they're afraid
Barb's getting too involved.
She might want a baby, too!

HELEN ~ preparations

Childbirth classes.
At the first one (Orientation)
the women introduce themselves
and their partners.
I have no partner.
I wish I was back home,
watching TV.

As we lie on the floor
during the relaxation class,
the midwife gushes,
"Imagine you are walking
into the waves, into the waves.
As each wave comes,
welcome the pain, welcome the pain!"
Everyone is smiling rapturously.
If Barb was here,
we'd have a good laugh.

The midwife is my partner
when we practice birth positions,
down on all fours,
or squatting.
The men are embarrassed.
Although they're trying to appear
committed and cool,
they are definitely glassy-eyed.
And I can tell
they'd like to be invisible

when the women talk openly of
hemorrhages,
the need to pee all the time,
and the urge to purge their bowels.

At the end of the classes
when the glowing mums-to-be
are drinking herbal tea,
the men escape—
they have to make a phone call,
or bring the car around,
or check if they have a parking ticket.
I'm out of there, too.

ironing

Mrs. Evans irons everything—
sheets, towels, pillowcases,
as well as everyone's clothes.
When Helen protests,
she says, "I enjoy it."
She doesn't tell Helen
that when she's ironing
she feels as if she's smoothing away
her troubles—
little problems,
big problems—
and by the end of the day
she has a satisfying pile
redolent with fresh air and sunshine.

sightings

From friends and acquaintances
there are reports of Leanne.
She's seen at a shopping center
in Burwood,
crossing a street in Maroubra,
lounging outside the Town Hall.
After each sighting,
Mrs. Evans is able to sleep a little,
give herself respite
from the awfulness
of waiting
to hear the worst.
Leanne may look very thin,
hair rough, skin blotchy,
but at least she's still alive.

HELEN ~ meeting

Mum keeps phoning Barb,
asking if I'm all right.
"She's worried about you," Barb says.
"She sounds desperate."
Through Barb,
I arrange to meet my mother
at a city coffee bar.
Her hair's a mess—the roots are dark,
and she has forgotten
to apply lipstick and nail polish.
"Celeste misses you terribly," she says.
"It's her birthday party next Saturday—
will you come?"
I raise my eyebrows.
"Does *Dad* know about this?"
She flushes.
"*I* want you to come. Please."
I imagine being in the living room,
my father looking at me,
his disgraceful, pregnant daughter.
His eyes will turn me to stone.

"Please, Hen?" says my mother.
"Don't call me that," I snap.
That name belongs
to younger, happier days,
when I thought my mother
was the most wonderful person
in the world.

HELEN ~ floating, unseen

Mum tries to give me money.
"For the baby," she says.
It's not her money.
It's my father's money.
"No," I say. "But thanks."

We sit for a long time in silence.
Mum's eyes are remote.
As if to herself, she says,
"The child died, you know.
I held him in my arms every day.
I sang to him.
I tried to bring him back."

I feel a cold shudder along my spine.
"What child?" I ask.
"What are you talking about?"

She tells me about the drowned boy,
floating, unseen, in a swimming pool,
while adults ate and drank
and laughed and joked,
in the friendly glow of party lights.

holding on

"Don't shut me out,"
Helen's mother says.
"Let me be a grandmother
to this baby."

Helen looks away.
She feels sorry for her mother.
But she also feels immensely weary.
She's just managing to hold on—
at the moment she can't face
dealing with her dad,
the whole family thing.
"Not yet," she says.

helen's parents

If they talked to each other,
he would ask,
"What do you do all day?"
She would say,
"I hold a drowned child in my arms."
If they talked to each other,
she would ask,
"What do you do all day?"
He would say,
"I am a man drowning."

helen's father

He knows he is inflexible,
but it's only now,
when he has nothing to do,
nowhere to go,
and is terrifyingly alone with himself,
that he finds himself dwelling
on why he is the way he is.

Perhaps only a child
of drug-abusing parents
knows what it's like to grow up
in chaos—
no routines,
no structures,
no rules,
no order,
no bedtimes,
no mealtimes.

He shudders at how
he and his brothers ran wild,
skipping school,
coming home when they liked,
existing on sandwiches and chips.

He was ten, at a friend's house,
confronted with knife and fork,
before he realized that not everyone
ate with their hands.

helen's mother

She has already lost one daughter,
and can see the other
turning into a replica of herself—
timid, eager to please,
shrinking from confrontation.

She is culpable.

HELEN ~ envy

Near the end
of the childbirth classes,
we have a guest mother.

Emily has come to tell her birth story.
She is sixteen.
Tiny miniskirt,
glowing skin,
no tummy.
The older mums groan with envy.

With her is her boyfriend
who looks as if he should be at home
doing his schoolwork.
But he is so casually expert
with his four-week-old baby,
the older dads groan with envy.

Emily says,
"I was going to have a water birth.
My dad hired a spa bath especially.
But as I was walking through the house,
the baby came in a rush—
so I had her
as I was holding on to the laundry tub,
surrounded by a week's washing!"
The boy laughs.
"She's such a clown!"
he says affectionately.

Emily laughs, too.
She pulls his hair.
"The neighborhood kids hopped into
the spa. They had a great time!"

The women envy Emily
her breeziness and flat stomach.
But I envy her the boy.

HELEN ~ baby shower

Barb organizes a party—
"a baby shower"—
at her house.
Her mum is there,
plus loads of girls from school.
They bring teddies, cute stuffed toys.
For the moment
I'm the center of attention,
more fascinating even than a pop star.

Everyone knows the old wives' tale—
carrying high, you're having a girl,
carrying low, you're having a boy.
As I'm carrying high,
they decide it's a girl.
I say nothing.
It's my secret,
mine and Raphael's.

They suggest their favorite names,
but no one speculates
who the baby will look like.
They're tactful,
and I'm grateful,
but I long to have Gabe here,
looking proud,
holding my hand.

HELEN ~ the dream

I run through
the darkening streets
with a tiny deformed man in my arms.
From a top window
comes an ugly shout,
"Christ, look at that monster!"
I veer away,
take another route,
duck into a building,
but there is no escape—
men dart out from nowhere
like cockroaches,
and tear
the tiny man from my arms.

still running

She wakes up,
heart jolting.
Raphael is rolling about,
a foot jabs her ribs.
"Just a dream," she says.
"Just a bad dream."
She strokes her stomach
and he quietens.
She thinks of him
    floating,
        sleeping.
He's safe, secure,
but she's still running
through the darkening streets.

HELEN ~ in the warm dark of me

Apparently, the unborn dream—
but what do they dream about?

Perhaps they dream of
unmapped lands, uncharted seas.
Perhaps they dream of worlds
fantastical.

In the warm dark of me,
I hope my child is dreaming
fearlessly.

HELEN ~ scared shitless!

On our day off,
Tony and I catch a bus to Bondi
for a paddle and an ice cream.
I lie on the sand
like a beached whale.

I gaze at the waves rolling in.
Welcome the pain, welcome the pain!
"I'm scared," I say.
It's not just fear of the pain.
There are humiliating bodily functions
I can't tell Tony about.
To put it bluntly,
I'm afraid I'll do a poo when I'm
pushing the baby out!
Tony pats my hand.
"I would say,
you are a very brave girl.
This baby will be proud
to have you as his mother."
Proud.
Proud of The Dish Pig.
I *will* make him proud of me
one day,
but right now
I'm scared shitless!

warm waters

Helen is scrubbing a pot
when her water breaks,
the warm fluid
gushing down her legs.
She stands, shocked,
in a puddle of water.

Tony helps her to a chair,
quickly mops the floor.
He says,
"I should call—right now!—
for an ambulance!"

She shakes her head,
sits quietly for a moment,
readying herself.

HELEN ~ goggling

Knees bent,
legs splayed
like an overcooked chicken.
Student doctors stroll in
to take a look.
This is the most humiliating
thing that's ever happened to me.
But soon I'm in such a red haze of pain
I no longer care
who goggles and gawks.

HELEN ~ pressure

The
   pressure
     is
       so
         great
          I'm
             scared
          I'm
         going
       to
     split
       and
         rip.

HELEN ~ bloody hell!

Women claim
you forget the agony
of childbirth.
Just as well.
This is far, far worse
than the most stabbing stomach cramps.
If the nurse dares to say,
"Welcome the pain,"
I'll bloody well belt her.
But she just says,
"Yell as much as you like, dear."
I need no encouragement.
I bellow so loudly
birds shoot out of the trees,
the earth splits open,
a tsunami towers over the harbor.
Grimly I vow
to keep my legs crossed in the future.
Raphael will just have to get used
to being an only child.

HELEN ~ not yet

I have a terrible urge
to push.
I just want to get the baby out,
get it over with.
The midwife says,
"Not yet! Not yet!"

HELEN ~ loop of pain

I've been in labor
for twelve hours now.
Groaning comes from
deep within me—
guttural,
growling.
I know it's *my* voice,
but it seems to belong
to someone else.
I am trapped
in a loop of pain—
on and on and on,
neverendingnever.
I am stuck.
The baby is stuck.
I've changed my mind.
I want to go home.

HELEN ～ naked

I'm kneeling in the shower,
leaning on a plastic chair.
The tiled floor is hard,
my knees are rubbed red and raw.
The water rippling
over my back is soothing.
We're all wet—me, the doctor,
the midwife, the nurse.
I'm so hot
I rip off my nightie,
leaving me naked
in front of strangers,
but I think,
What the hell!
They've seen it all before.

HELEN ~ courage

The midwife says,
"You can do it."
She is so encouraging,
so sure,
that I take a deep breath,
summon up courage,
send it coursing
to the far reaches
of my body.

HELEN ~ he is beautiful

I give one last grinding
push.
The baby slides out.
I feel a shock of relief
as the pain stops.
I can't bear to look.
"Is he all right?" I whisper.
By this I mean,
is his face all right?
The midwife says,
"He's perfect.
Ten fingers, ten toes."

I'm trembling like a leaf.
The nurse helps me totter
to a low bed.
She lays my baby on my stomach.
He is gulping.
He is bright purple.
He is beautiful.

I
  fall
    passionately
      irrevocably
        in
          love.

HELEN ~ my baby

He is warm and damp,
squirmy,
with arms and legs jerking,
flailing in strange space.
His eyes are shut,
his face grimaces,
his mouth makes little sucking noises.
We are still linked by a cord
as thick as my finger,
but even when it's clamped and cut,
I know we will always be roped
together.

Now, wrapped up tightly,
he lies against my heart.
I hope he hears it beating,
strong and steadfast,
as he did in the nourishing dark of my body.

HELEN ~ shared joy

In the ward
I'm the only one without
family or a husband or boyfriend.
I have visitors—
Barb,
Tony,
Mr. Scroop (for three seconds),
even Mrs. Evans.
She won't hold Raphael,
or look at him.
She obviously dislikes babies.

When the visitors go,
the dads stay on.
I see
closeness,
caresses,
shared joy.
I switch off my light,
and draw the curtains around my bed.

After a day and a half,
I pack my bag,
sign myself out,
take Raphael to the boardinghouse.

HELEN ~ breathing

Every half hour
I tiptoe into my room
to check that Raphael is still breathing.

I prod him.
If he twitches or stirs,
I breathe more easily,
then creep away,
now desperate not to wake him.

At the doorway
I try to remember to take a giant step
over the loose floorboard
that cracks like thunder.

This time I forget.
The floorboard booms.
I hold my breath,
cursing.
But I'm lucky.
Raphael sleeps on.

breast-feeding

Raphael won't breast-feed.
He just can't get the hang
of latching onto a nipple.

Helen's breasts harden.
A rocky outcrop,
so sore she can hardly
move her arms.

Mrs. Evans makes Raphael a bottle,
and persuades Helen to stuff her bra
with fresh cabbage leaves.
She smells like a vegetable garden,
but it works.

She tries breast-feeding again.
Raphael cries for the bottle.
Helen feels like a failure.

HELEN ∼ no one warned me

Breast-feeding
is not all it's cracked up to be.
Might be good for the baby,
but there's either a gush of milk
or not enough.
And no one warned me
the sucking is painful.
I grit my teeth
as Raphael at last consents
to champ me.
But he won't touch my left breast—
it is small, while the other is so huge
it could knock someone off their feet.

HELEN ~ sleep

Sleep deprivation—
there's nothing worse—
no wonder torturers love it!

My body craves sleep,
unbroken sleep,
sleep of centuries,
sleep of the dead.
It's all I think about.

I stand dully
by the cot,
my arms hanging by my sides.
I don't know if I have the strength
to pick him up,
to rock him,
to stop the awful endless howling.

HELEN ~ weeping

Raphael wakes in the night
for the third time.
I shove my head under the pillow,
and chant, "Go back to sleep,"
but he doesn't.

I crawl out of bed,
look at him with despair.
I check his diaper,
offer him a bottle,
try singing a lullaby,
but my voice cracks.
And still he cries,
on and on and on.
"Please stop it," I whimper.
"Please. Please. Please!"
But he just thrashes his arms and legs.
I take him into bed with me.
We're both weeping now,
as if our hearts will break.
And that's how Mrs. Evans finds us.

friends

Mrs. Evans helps
look after Raphael
so Helen can rest.
She sterilizes bottles,
makes up feeds,
pats the baby to sleep.

The three of them go on outings to
the park,
the plant shop,
the supermarket.
Helen is amazed at how much
Mrs. Evans can pack
into her tiny cane basket.
It's bottomless!
Mrs. Evans laughs.
"When I was a young girl
I was a packer in a factory."
A few weeks ago,
Helen would have found it hard
to imagine
this dried-up old woman
ever being young,
but now she talks with her as easily
as she used to with Barb.

luscious as plums

Mrs. Evans loves holding the baby,
loves the warm weight of him
on her shoulder,
loves his plump little legs,
luscious as plums,
loves how he burrows into her
as she carries him to bed,
loves the abandon of his sleep,
arms outflung,
hands unfurled
like morning flowers.

HELEN ~ granddaughter

Mrs. Evans tells me about
her granddaughter, Leanne.
"She stole whatever I had—
TV, video, credit cards.
She didn't care,
she needed the money.
The drugs made her happy.

I helped her find
somewhere to live.
She didn't pay rent,
and ended up on the streets
with a plastic bag of clothes.
She phoned me at midnight.

On the train to the city
we sat next to each other
like strangers.
I was her jailer,
I was taking her to detox."

HELEN ~ play group

I go to a mothers' group,
but the women are much older
than me,
smarter,
better educated,
with jobs to go back to.
Their babies are designer-dressed,
the strollers are as big as cars.
They talk about
husbands,
mortgages,
holidays,
even their sex lives.
I say little.
When the babies need feeding,
the women unbutton their blouses
with milky complacency.
They glance at each other
as I produce a bottle.
I know they are thinking,
That poor baby!
Doesn't the silly girl
understand breast milk is better?

I won't ever go back.

HELEN ~ so delectable

After his bath,
Raphael nestles on my stomach,
soft and succulent.
I stroke his tiny hands,
the fingernails like specks of cream.
I caress his silky head,
the bones delicate, delicious.
I pat his plump puppy tummy.
He's so delectable
I could eat him up!

HELEN ~ generosity

Mrs. Evans halves my rent.
"Don't argue," she says.
"Babies cost money."
She hands me a pile of folded diapers.
"When you're ready
to go back to *school*,
I'll mind Raphael for you.
No charge."
Her generosity is so overwhelming
I burst into tears.
Raphael gets a fright.
His mouth starts to wobble.
"That's enough of that, you two,"
orders Mrs. Evans.
"It's not charity, Helen.
When you're a famous surgeon
you can pay me back."
"I will," I promise. "I will."

HELEN ~ hot blue sky

We lie on the grass,
Mrs. Evans, Raphael, and I.
Raphael stares up at the clouds.
He gurgles,
kicks his legs,
waves.
Mrs. Evans laughs,
but I can tell she is wistful,
remembering.
"Ever since she was little,
Leanne's favorite thing
was to watch the sky changing.
Nothing made her happier
than a hot blue sky."

cold drinks

At Christmas,
Tony usually goes home
to the Philippines,
but this year
he buys a fridge
for his family instead.

He speaks to his mother
on the phone.
She says his little brothers and sisters
are so excited they can't sleep.
They've never had cold drinks before.
And already all the neighbors
are asking if they may
put *their* meat and drinks in the fridge.

"I would say,
this present is a great success,"
Tony says to Helen.
But he's fighting back the tears,
and she can do nothing
except hug his slight body,
and tell him he's the sweetest man
she's ever met.

christmas day

On Christmas Day,
Mrs. Evans sets an extra place
at the table,
in case Leanne should turn up.
Mr. Scroop asks her
to set a place, too, for his son.
He is sure *this* year
he will come.

Mrs. Evans usually finds Christmas
dismal.
But today,
a lopsided pine tree makes the house
smell like a forest,
and she has company around the table,
even though Helen is subdued,
and Tony is gusty with sighs.

Mrs. Evans enjoys everyone's delight
as they discover old silver coins
in the Christmas pudding,
but she knows the air of festivity
is as fragile
as the translucent glass ornaments
suspended
on the tree.

In the evening,
Mr. Scroop, his heart sore,

rushes off for a quick walk.
Tony and Helen listen to music,
their fingers linked,
and Mrs. Evans rocks Raphael to sleep,
his soft, downy head
against her cheek.

HELEN ∼ mr. scroop's son

I ask Mrs. Evans,
"Shouldn't we try to contact
Mr. Scroop's son?
There must be an address or
phone number."

Mrs. Evans looks at me silently.
Then she says,
"There is no son.
He died a long time ago.
Mr. Scroop refuses to remember."

washing day

Mrs. Evans is taking down
the laundry
when she keels over.
Pegs, bright as children's toys,
scatter to the ground.

From the kitchen window,
Mr. Scroop sees her fall.
He rushes into the garden,
rushes back into the house,
calls for an ambulance,
waits,
jiggling on the spot,
until it comes and takes
Mrs. Evans away,
then he rushes out into the street
to look for Helen,
but she's nowhere to be found.

He sits alone in the house,
his feet still,
his hands folded in his lap,
as memories come bursting in.

HELEN ~ waiting

That night
Mr. Scroop and I sit in the kitchen,
and wait.
There is no smell of fresh ironing
in the air,
no fragrant meal simmering on the stove.
Mr. Scroop is crying,
fists in his eyes, like a child,
but there's nothing childlike
about the ugly sobs
that wrench his body.

I call the hospital again.
I tell Mr. Scroop,
"She's not going to die.
She's very ill,
but she's going to be all right.
She will be coming home."

Mr. Scroop rubs his face.
He whispers,
"My son will not call.
My son will not come.
My son is dead."

I stroke his neck.
"I'm so sorry, Mr. Scroop."

HELEN ~ the promise

Mrs. Evans is paralyzed down one side,
her face is twisted,
her speech garbled.
I can't make out what she's saying,
so I ask a nurse for a pen and paper.

Mrs. Evans scribbles a message:
"Please find Leanne.
Tell her I've given up the cigarettes."

I promise, "I will."
I'll hunt through the city streets,
down lanes, down alleys.
I'll show Leanne's photo to buskers and beggars.
I'll ask derelicts on park benches, in doorways.
I'll search day and night
until I find her.

But to do this,
I need someone to take care of Raphael.

HELEN ∼ no choice

I wheel the stroller home,
along an avenue of trees.
Raphael is entranced
by the play of light on leaves.
At any other time,
I would enjoy the rapture on his face.

Who can I leave him with?
Tony is elbow-deep in dishwater at work,
Mr. Scroop is too sad to cope,
Barb and her parents have gone camping.
There's my mother . . .
but she's a stranger now,
and, anyway, she'd try to stop me.

I have no choice.
I must go into alien territory.

HELEN ∼ preparations

I bathe Raphael,
loving his soft, slippery body.
"I won't be away long,"
I tell him.
"I will come back, come back, come back."
My promise turns into a song,
and I keep on singing it,
reassuring myself
as much as him.

I pack the baby bag
(Raphael has more equipment
than a rock star),
and phone Gabe's house
to make sure they're home.
Sara answers.
"Sorry," I say. "Wrong number."
I give Raphael a big hug—
"Daddy's waiting!"

HELEN ~ all right

I nearly press the bell
three times
to stop the bus and get off.
Raphael's fussy,
but falls asleep in the stroller
on the way to Gabe's house.

I knock on the door.
Wait.
As soon as I hear footsteps
thumping down the stairs,
I run out of the gate,
and duck behind a parked car,
listening for the door to open.
I can't bear to see Gabe.
He told me that night how nice
Sara is.
She'll look after Raphael
for the weekend.
He'll be all right, all right, all right.

Gabe & HELEN

GABE ~ the baby

We're partying at my house tonight
as my family's just taken off
to visit Grandpop
for a couple of days.
It's too good an opportunity
to miss.

I open the front door,
expecting to see Bram or Al,
but there's a stroller on the doorstep.
In it is a baby.
Huh?
I glance around,
saunter down the steps,
look up and down the street.
Nothing. No one.
I go back to the stroller,
stare at the baby.
It must belong to some friend
of Sara's.
The baby opens its eyes.
Yawns.
Smiles.
I feel the hairs rising
on the back of my neck.

GABE ～ the note

I peer into the stroller.
Pinned to the baby's blanket
is a note.
"Sara—
I have to do something
very important.
Please look after Raphael
until Sunday evening.
He's Gabe's son, too."

The note is unsigned.

I feel as if I've been
slammed in the head,
punched in the stomach,
chopped off at the knees.

GABE ~ so many girls

When I've persuaded
my legs to work,
I pull the stroller into the house.
If this *is* my kid,
who's the mother?
There've been so many parties,
so many girls.

I bury my head in my hands.
The baby laughs.
It thinks I'm playing peekaboo.

too late, mate

Gabe props Raphael on his knee,
shakily phones Bram and Al
to come over immediately.

Al stares in awe at the baby,
but Bram is staring at Gabe,
despising
his stupidity and carelessness.
Eventually he says,
"You must have some idea
who the kid's mother is."
There is contempt in his voice.
Gabe flushes,
shakes his head,
mutters,
"We'll have to cancel the party."
"Too late, mate," Al says.
Bram agrees.
"Your problem, Gabe.
It goes ahead as planned."

HELEN ~ looking for leanne

I sit on the Town Hall steps,
trying not to be trampled
by eager people meeting up
with friends.
I work out my strategy—
cinemas,
pinball parlors,
railway stations,
bus stops,
parks,
cafés.

My chances are slight,
but someone, somewhere,
may have seen Leanne.
Someone, somewhere,
may know something.

in the dark

It is nightfall
when Helen trudges away
from the bright shopping centers,
and enters the dark.
This is not the exhilarating blackness
of a country sky,
or the mysterious darkness
threading trees in a forest.
This is the blurriness
of scraggy streets,
boarded-up windows,
abandoned cars,
smashed beer bottles.

A shadow detaches itself
from a doorway.
A drunk pisses against a wall.
A child shrieks.

Helen quakes.
Only the grief in Mrs. Evans's eyes
keeps her going.
She grips the strap of her backpack,
and walks purposefully.
She shows the photo
to everyone she encounters.
"Have you seen this woman?"
No one has.
No one cares to ask, "Why?"

nothing

Later that night,
Helen calls
refuges, boardinghouses,
youth centers, drug centers.

Nothing.

She thinks of chalking a message
on pavements and walls.
She thinks of writing on billboards.
She thinks of painting a message
so large
Leanne may well see it. . . .

HELEN ~ the request

I call home.
It's very late.
My mother answers
almost immediately,
her voice apprehensive.
"It's me," I say.
"I need your help."
I tell her precisely what I want,
expecting her to reply,
"I'll have to ask your father."
But she simply says,
"Leave it to me."

GABE ~ not the coolest

I'm not the coolest guy
at the party—
I have puke on my shoulder,
dribble on my collar,
banana gunk in my hair.
But at last Raphael's asleep
in my bed,
barricaded with pillows.
I keep on running upstairs
to make sure he hasn't rolled off
or isn't crying.

the swarm

Al has been boozing all evening—
pouring anything and everything
down his throat.
His head buzzes.
It's as if a swarm of bees
has made him their hive.
He shakes his head,
but this only makes the bees angrier.
"Fuck," he mutters.

No one sees him lurch up the stairs.
No one sees him push open the door
to Gabe's room.
No one hears his crazy giggle.

one night

One night
a drunken boy sways
on the stairs.
It is shadowy on the stairs.
The stairs are narrow and steep.
The boy is holding something
in his hands.
He is going to throw it
across the room.
He believes it to be a football,
but this football is soft and warm.
Its heart beats.

GABE ~ catch!

Someone calls,
"Hey, Gabe! Catch!"

It is Al.
Goblin-shadow on the stairs.
Hands huge,
as in a distorted close-up.
He is jiggling Raphael.

In a lightning
            flash
                I remember—
Al at Chris's party, his eyes dazed,
the melon sailing across the room
smashing against the wall
orange pulp
    juice
        pips
            splattering—

Raphael wails.

"No!" I shout.
"Al! Don't!"

something terrible

Just before
something terrible happens,
time seems to
stop.
In the stillness,
onlookers see the future—
the imminent terrifying future—
then they are yanked back
into the present,
with only seconds
to stop
the future
from happening.

GABE ∼ drunken bastard

I am trapped in slow motion,
the blood in my veins
thick and sluggish.
My brain is screaming,
but my arms and legs merely
churn and chug.

Al is raising the baby,
getting ready to throw.

Bram tears past me.
He leaps up the stairs,
grabs Raphael,
thrusts him at me,
then leans over the banister,
retching.

Al looks as if he has been slammed
awake.
He sinks to his knees,
clinging to the railings.
"Jeez!" he whispers. "Jeez!"

I stare at him,
words choking in my throat.
Raphael is sobbing.

Bram spits,
wipes his mouth
with the back of his hand.
He is trembling.
"You fucking drunken bastard!
You nearly killed the kid!"

into the night

Gabe wraps Raphael in a jacket,
and runs into the night.
He runs without breathing,
without his feet touching the ground.

He runs to the corner shop,
hammers on the door.
After what feels like a century,
Gino opens it,
his annoyance turning to alarm.
He pulls Gabe into the shop
and goes to fetch Christina,
but it is Uncle who arrives first,
and silently puts his arms around
Gabe and the baby.

While Raphael sleeps
in Uncle's bed,
Gabe and Uncle sit in the kitchen
and talk.

end of the party

The partygoers melt away.
Some of the girls are crying,
the boys look sick.
Bram and the clean-up crew
start setting the house to rights.
They work fast and silently.
They can't wait to leave
this place
where something tragic
almost happened.

because of him

Bram is the last
to leave.
He checks his photographs and notes.
Everything is in place.
Everything is in order.

He shuts the door,
starts trudging home.
It will take him hours,
but as long as he concentrates on
one step after another,
he can shut out the thoughts,
shut out the knowledge
that it is *he*,
not Al,
who desired damage.

obliteration

Al walks into the traffic,
disregarding
the squeal
and stink
of burning rubber,
the blasting horns,
the shouting of drivers,
first petrified, then furious.
He deserves to be flattened.
Wiped out.
Obliterated.

go home

Outside the caravan park,
Bram stops to address
the ravens.
"It's over," he says.
"Go home."
Malice and Envy stare at him.
He feels the full force
of their intelligence.
"The parties were stupid.
Pointless.
Okay?
Now leave me alone."
One of the birds lets out
a rasping croak,
then, with a flap of its wings,
it is gone.
But the other stays.
Bram doesn't know if it is
Malice or Envy.

sick

Al is shivering.
Sick.
He can smell the booze
oozing
from the pores of his skin.
He tears off his clothes,
fills up the bath,
lies in it like a dead fish.

He searches for
clean jeans, a shirt,
then bundles up his old coat,
and goes into the night
to stuff it in the bin.
The suburb is sleeping,
but he feels as if
he is just beginning to wake.

next morning

In the morning
Baby Boboli is thrilled
to find Gabe and a *baby*
snuggled up in Uncle's bed.
"Did Santa come *again*?" she asks.

She's convinced that somehow
she's acquired a new baby brother.
She insists that she and Uncle accompany
Gabe home
to change and feed Raphael.

Then the four of them go to the
children's park.
Baby Boboli shouts to Raphael,
"Baby, Baby, watch me!"
as she performs
on the slide and the seesaw and the swing.
She can't wait for him to walk and talk.

AL ~ blood, flesh, and bone

In my hands
I held a football—
In my hands
I held blood, flesh, and bone—

I could cut off my hands,
but the memory of what I did
will never be excised.

HELEN ~ the message

Sunday morning.
The sky is
clear,
hot blue,
irresistible.

In the back garden,
Mr. Scroop, Tony, and I
watch a plane—
tiny as the tip of a pencil—
begin to write.

It
soars,
plunges,
loops,
and swoops,
until
the words hang white,
pegged momentarily in the sky
LEANNE PHONE HOME
then begin to blur and fade.

"I would say," says Tony,
"every girl named Leanne
may now phone home!"
"Let's hope ours does,"
says Mr. Scroop.

He rushes off
to sit by the phone,
and is still there
at midnight
when at last
it rings.

the homecoming

Raphael is asleep
in Gabe's bed
when the family returns home.

While Luke is in the toolshed,
Gabe tells them everything—
the parties,
the one-night stands,
the unknown girl,
the baby,
the almost-disaster.

Sara sits motionless,
her arms wrapped around
her body
as if she is trying
to keep herself warm.
Gabe's father clenches
and unclenches his fists.
Gabe braces himself.
But his father simply says,
"I'm so ashamed of you.
So very ashamed."

GABE ~ the girl

I open the door warily.
A girl and I stare at each other.
"Who are you?"
But already I know.
She's that girl from a party,
a year ago,
the girl who saw into my soul,
the girl who had a smile
that transformed her face.
She's smiling now.
She is beautiful.
"At the café
they called me The Dish Pig,
but my name is Helen."
"Helen," I repeat.
"Helen of Gordon."
I remember the phone calls,
remember shouting at Sara
to tell some girl I'd left the country.
"I'm sorry," I say.
"So am I," she says.
The smile vanishes.
She doesn't look sorry.
She looks fierce.
She looks like a mother lion
who wants her cub back.

HELEN ~ meet the family

Gabe takes me
into the living room.
"This is Helen," he mutters.
A man heaves himself off the sofa,
offers me his seat.
Sara gets up, too.
She puts her arms around me,
as if she's known me all my life.
A small boy looks up
from a vast contraption of pipes
running under the coffee table,
around the sofa,
along the walls.
He holds up a piece of plastic.
"This is called an elbow," he says.
"Did you know that?"
I bend down,
examine the pipe.
"No," I say. "But it's a good name for it."
The boy nods, pleased.
"Come on, Luke," says his father.
"Let's see what else we can find
in the shed."
"Raphael's asleep," says Sara.
"When you're ready, I'll bring him in."
"I'm ready now," I say.

GABE ~ don't go

Helen settles Raphael into the stroller.
"Home time," she says.
Raphael waves a fat little fist.
She smiles at him.

God, I love that smile!

"Don't go," I blurt out.

Helen releases the brakes on the stroller.
She looks at me coldly.
"I don't know if I like you, Gabe.
I don't even know you."

I catch her hand.
"Can I see you again?" I ask.
"And Raphael?
Please."

helen's dad

One rainy morning
when he's pretending
to go to work,
he sees a rainbow
dancing
down the street.
Like a child,
he rubs his eyes—and sees
it is an umbrella
of such dazzling brilliance
his heart leaps.
He runs after the rainbow,
but it vanishes
into the fog.

walking home

He walks home,
rain running down his face
like tears.
He walks home to tell his wife
about the rainbow dancing
in the street.
He walks home to tell his wife
about his lost job.
He walks home to tell his wife
he is lost.

HELEN ~ rapid recovery

Mrs. Evans gets well fast.
She's scared of nursing homes.
She tells me why.

A stroke took
her husband's mobility, his speech.
He was convalescing in a nursing home
of apparently good repute.

One summer morning
a young nurse wheeled him
into the garden for a few minutes' sun,

and forgot him.

Mrs. Evans weeps again now,
remembering his raw face and head and hands.
"No one admitted responsibility,
and he was mute, he was *mute*."

miracles

Mrs. Evans has never believed in miracles,
but they are happening
around her.
She has recovered from her stroke.
Leanne is trying to put her life back together.
Even the veranda seems to have changed
its mind about running away—
the gap is closing and the front door
is opening once again.
But the biggest miracle of all
is happening to Mrs. Evans's heart—
it beats so strongly and loudly
with love
for Leanne and Helen and Raphael
that she wakes each day rejoicing.

the gift

Barb delivers an old quilt,
soft cotton with a teddy bear print,
faded and darned.
Helen holds it to her face,
breathes in,
remembering.
Her mother has written,
"You've probably forgotten
your old baby blanket.
But you loved it—nearly to bits!
Perhaps Raphael will love it, too?"

dark forest

Leanne is on a farm,
working so hard
she falls into bed,
not waking until morning
when cows bump against
the walls of the house.

Dark forest borders the farm,
but Leanne shuns it,
afraid to stray along paths
away from the clear glare of light.

the sky

Leanne dreams
she holds the sky in her hands,
her thumbprints smudge it
brown and grey.
She wipes it clean
with a soft white cloth
until it is shining blue.

She sits on her hands,
resolved to leave the sky alone,
but, oh, how she yearns
to touch it!

gabe's heart

"Does he have a good heart?"
asks Mrs. Evans.
Helen thinks of the empty
chambers of Gabe's heart,
of the crucial missing valves.
She thinks, too,
of how his heart is regenerating,
growing muscle,
feeding hungry cells.
"He will," she says.
Mrs. Evans switches off the iron,
and gives Helen a bundle of clothing,
warm as a sleeping child.
"Then all is possible."

the image

Al has grown up in a house
where his parents do not touch,
do not speak.
"They hate each other,"
he used to whisper to his toys.

One morning,
Al opens
the door to their room,
and finds them asleep, naked,
arms and legs entwined.
He tiptoes away,
his heart galloping.

He lies in bed,
unsure if he dreamed this,
or if it really happened.
But he wants to believe,
wants to hold on to this image
for the rest of his life.

reading

Helen's mother dreams
she is reading
to a sleeping girl,
a girl in a coma,
her perfect face as blank as a doll's.

Helen's mother reads
fairy tales and folktales
about quests and journeys and triumphs.
She reads story after story,
from beginning to end.
"The beginnings are best,"
she tells the girl,
"with their promise of things to come."

gabe's dad

Without bitterness,
he tells Gabe
why "the mermaid"
agreed to marry him.

"I was renting a house with a pool—
the filter didn't work properly,
the surface was scummy,
but she lay in it all day, soaking.
In water
she glistened.
In dry air
she faded, was lackluster."

Gabe asks,
"Did she really love
the old guy with the yacht?"
His father grimaces.
"I hope so.
Or perhaps it was the promise
of never-ending water
she couldn't resist."

the drifter

Gabe's mother fled
from a dusty country town,
where people prayed for rain,
to a city on the harbor.
She craved water,
needed it to feel alive.
She took a job as a mermaid
so she could stare out to sea
without interruption.

She drifted
from acting to modeling to marriage.
She was snagged down
by a child
for a while,
then—happily—found herself
a benevolent man
who would sail her away
in a luxury yacht.

She travels the tropics,
soaking up sunny waters,
but she will never venture
into cold, dark depths.
She will never know
what marvels there might be
at the bottom of the sea.

GABE ～ it is time

I reach under my bed,
pull out the box,
blow away the dust.
It is time to open
the envelopes,
read the letters,
let my mother speak.

HELEN ~ studying again

I've re-enrolled
at correspondence school.
Those brown envelopes
are thumping into the mailbox again.
They are no longer quite so fat,
or quite so daunting.

Mrs. Evans, Tony, and Mr. Scroop
are always nagging me
to go and study.
I know they want me to do well—
but they also want to run off
with Raphael and play!

helen's father

Helen's father gets another job—
he has contacts,
belongs to a business network.
Not for him
the humiliation of
the unemployment line.
But he doesn't forget
the bleak days in the park.

new beginnings

Helen's mother does something
she's always wanted—
enrolls at the university to study nursing.

Celeste beams.
"Now I can go to After School Care!"
Many of her friends go,
and she feels she's been missing out.

Helen's father manages
to hide his dismay
at this disruption to his home life.
He opens a bottle of champagne,
and toasts his wife.
"To new beginnings—
and the promise of things to come."

meeting the grandparents

Helen takes Raphael
to meet his grandparents
and aunt.
Celeste loves being an aunt.
She's the only aunt at school.
This distinction makes her feel
quite grown-up.

Helen's mother says,
"We wondered if you'd like
to come and live at home.
We could turn the spare bedroom
into a nursery."

Helen glances at her father.
He's trying not to look self-conscious
as he plays with Raphael's toes
in a game of This Little Piggy Went to Market.
He smiles at Helen.
"What color would you like it painted?"

HELEN ~ moving on

I can't go back to live
with my mum and dad.
I want to be free
to lead my own life,
to bring Raphael up the way
I see fit.

"I'll visit," I promise.
My mother takes my hand.
"I'm happy to babysit," she says,
"whenever you like."
My father opens his mouth,
then shuts it.
Raphael's toes are getting
a good old tweaking,
but he doesn't mind.

GABE ~ raphael and al

While Helen is studying,
I look after Raphael.
His toys are beginning to colonize
the house.
I ask Al over.
He sidles into the room,
won't look at the baby.
"Pick him up," I say,
but he mutters, "I can't."
I reach over,
and plonk Raphael in Al's lap.
Al flinches.
Raphael grabs Al's hair,
waves a fat little fist.
Al smiles.
"That's right," he says,
"punch me on the nose, big guy!"

GABE ~ dad's party

When my dad was a kid,
he desperately wanted a birthday party,
but his parents just never bothered.
Now, on his forty-fifth birthday,
Sara organizes a surprise party—
a kid's party for the oldies!
"Since you're such an expert on parties,"
Sara says to me,
"you can be in charge of the games."
I go to the library,
borrow a book on party games for
five-to-eight-year-olds,
and talk Helen into coming along
as a Helpful Helper.

GABE ~ the big day!

Sara makes
sausage rolls, hot chips, iced cupcakes,
fairy bread, funny-face biscuits,
chocolate mud cake.

There's Coke, fizzy drinks, orange squash,
jelly, ice cream, chocolate frogs.

The adults fall on the feast
with cries of glee.
Before long there's a food fight.
Luke is shocked.
"You'll get into big trouble!"
Sara warns them,
"If you don't behave,
you won't get lollies to take home."
That scares them.
They're as good as gold—
for five minutes.
Sara nips into the kitchen,
adds rum to her Coke.
Helen is laughing so much
she's an Unhelpful Helper.
As punishment,
she has to wipe
everyone's sticky fingers.

I get them organized for
Pass the Parcel,
Follow the Leader,
Statues,
Musical Chairs.
Mrs. Bartley from next door
has a good old time plonking herself
on men's laps.
Sara has to have a quiet word with her.

After the guests have gone home,
grubby but happy,
clutching their party favors,
Dad grabs Sara
and kisses her thoroughly.
"Thanks, love," he says.
"That was the bestest party ever!"
"Grow up," I growl.
He grins.
"Next year I want clowns and a magician!"

HELEN ~ grunt, piggy, grunt

That was the first "kids" party
I didn't watch from the sidelines.
Before my face was fixed,
I dreaded the game
Piggy in the Middle.
It had nothing to do with pigs,
of course,
just kids throwing a ball
over the head of the one in the middle,
but I felt everyone was looking at me.

I tell Gabe this.
He hugs me,
kisses the tip of my nose.
I snort.
He snorts.
Luke shakes his head,
and looks at us pityingly.

back at school

Al is back at school,
trying to pass this time.
To his surprise,
the girls don't mind
sitting next to him,
and he even has
a couple of new friends.
He's not making any plans
for the future,
just focusing on the here and now,
trying to get it right.

heading home

Gabe scraped
into university
and is enrolled in Arts.
He has no idea
what he will do with his life.
He often dreams about
Helen and Raphael,
but, once, most peculiarly,
he dreams
he is eel larvae
floating across seas,
heading home.

He wakes
in a sheen of salty sweat,
and lies quietly,
wondering.

the bird

Bram is on a scholarship at university,
studying economics,
involved in student politics.
The only trouble is,
he often thinks there's a bird perched
on his shoulder,
but no one else can see it.

the three of them

The three of them sometimes meet
for coffee at a friendly café
where no one hurries them along.
"So," says Al, "are we all still fucked up?"
"Fucked if I know," says Bram.
"Hope the fuck not," says Gabe.
"Hey," says a waitress,
"watch your fucking language, you guys!"
The three of them laugh, remembering.
"Sorry, miss," says Al,
his eyes as bright as river stones.

HELEN ~ small steps

After his university lectures,
Gabe comes over
and we take Raphael
to the park.
It makes me laugh
how the other mums
can hardly keep their hands off Gabe—
they think it's wonderful
this gorgeous young man
takes such tender care of his baby.

I have no problem
keeping my hands to myself.
I'm not sure how I feel about Gabe.
I'm just taking
small, slow steps
until I know
the foundations are sound.

h e n

Helen and her mother
are playing with Raphael
in the back garden.
Her mother says softly,
"It's good to have you here, Hen."
This time Helen smiles
and accepts her childhood name.

"Hey," she says,
"you never mentioned that
the Tasmanian hen
has huge, muscular legs
and makes an awful noise!"

Her mother laughs.
"Your mum's a tough little bird,"
she tells Raphael.
"Never forget that."

well-wishing

Last Saturday in summer,
Johnstone Park Aquatic Center,
Gabe, Uncle, Baby Boboli, Raphael.
Gabe sits in the shallow babies' pool,
his son tucked between his legs.
Raphael smacks the water, astonished
when drops fall on his head
like rain.
Baby Boboli lies on her tummy,
kicking furiously.
"I'm swimming!" she signs to Uncle.
Uncle signs back, "Well done!"

Somewhere a child wails,
and Gabe recalls
that summer afternoon
when he observed
the sullen girl,
the weary woman,
and the crying baby.
He glances around,
not really expecting to see them,
but wanting to wish them well.